WALT DISNEY PRODUCTIONS

presents

TOD and VIXEY

FROM *The Fox and the Hound*

Random House  New York

Book Club Edition

Copyright © 1981 by Walt Disney Productions. All rights reserved under International and Pan-American Copyright Conventions. Published in the United States by Random House, Inc., New York, and simultaneously in Canada by Random House of Canada Limited, Toronto.

Library of Congress Cataloging in Publication Data: Main entry under title: Walt Disney Productions presents Tod and Vixey from the Fox and the hound. (Disney's wonderful world of reading ; 50) SUMMARY: A domesticated fox's lonely exile to a game preserve is lightened when he meets a friendly lady fox named Vixey. [1. Foxes—Fiction] I. Mannix, Daniel Pratt, 1911-   . Fox and the hound. II. Walt Disney Productions.   III. Title.   IV. Title: Tod and Vixey from the Fox and the hound.   V. Series.   PZ7.T564 [E]   81-5209 ISBN: 0-394-84904-3 (trade); 0-394-94904-8 (lib. bdg.) AACR2

Manufactured in the United States of America   A B C D E F G H I J K   2 3 4 5 6 7 8 9 0

Once there was a young fox who met
a hound pup in the woods.
The fox liked that pup right away.

The fox and the hound became good friends.
Every day they played together.
They did not know that foxes and hounds
could not be friends forever.

The fox was named Tod.
He lived with a kind farmer
named Mrs. Tweed.
Mrs. Tweed loved Tod and
took good care of him.

The hound pup was named Copper.
He lived with a bad-tempered hunter
named Amos Slade.
Amos had plans for Copper.

Amos took Copper away.
He taught Copper how to be a hunting dog.
He showed Copper how to track animals.

When Copper came back,
he would not play with Tod.

"I am a hunting dog now,"
said Copper. "I hunt foxes!"
Tod ran home scared.

Amos saw Tod leave.

"What was that fox doing here?"
yelled Amos. "I bet he wants
my chickens!"

Amos hopped in
his car and went
to see Mrs. Tweed.

"Your fox is trying to steal my chickens!"
yelled Amos through the door.

"Go away!" said Mrs. Tweed.
"Tod would not steal a thing."

"If you don't get rid of that fox,"
said Amos, "I will!"
He got in his car and went home.

"Tod is not safe
on my farm anymore,"
thought Mrs. Tweed.
"I must find him
a new place to live."

The next day she put Tod
in her car and drove away.

They drove along until they came to the game preserve.

The game preserve was a big park where hunting was not allowed.

Many kinds of wild animals lived
in the game preserve.

"Stay here, Tod," said Mrs. Tweed.
"This is your new home."

Mrs. Tweed drove away.
She felt terrible.
Tod felt terrible, too.
He was alone and scared.
He did not like this strange new place.

It began to rain.
Soon Tod was cold
and wet.
"I need a dry place
to spend the night,"
he thought.

The fox ran through the woods—
not really knowing where to look.

Tod peeked inside a hollow tree.
Oops! That tree was already taken.

Next he saw a nice dry nest in the ground.
But a badger already lived there.
"Scram!" said the badger. "Beat it!"

A little porcupine poked his head out of
a hole in a tree.

"Do you want to come in here?" he said.

"Gee, thanks!" said Tod.

The porcupine's nest
was dry and warm.
Tod was happy
to sleep there.

But Tod was not so happy in the morning.
The porcupine woke up and stretched.
His sharp quills pricked Tod.

"Ouch!" cried Tod.
He left quickly.

Tod set off to explore his new home.

He was very lonely.

He missed Mrs. Tweed and Copper.

"Hi!" said a nice friendly voice.
Tod turned around.
There was another fox!
"I'm Vixey," she said. "Who are you?"
"My name is Tod," said Tod shyly.

Tod liked Vixey right away.

Soon the two foxes were good friends.

Vixey took Tod to her burrow.
"Why do you have two doors?"
asked Tod.
"When you are a fox," said Vixey,
"you have to be ready for trouble."
And sure enough, trouble was
on the way.

GAME
PRESERVE
NO HUNTING

Amos Slade brought Copper
to the game preserve.
He paid no attention to
the NO HUNTING signs.
He wanted to hunt!

ABSOLUTELY
NO
HUNTING!

Copper began to sniff around.
Soon he was on the track of something.
"Good boy!" said Amos.

Copper led Amos straight to Vixey's burrow!

"Foxes!" said Amos. "I will smoke them out."
He built a fire at one door of the burrow.

Smoke began to fill the burrow.
"We must get out of here!" said Tod.

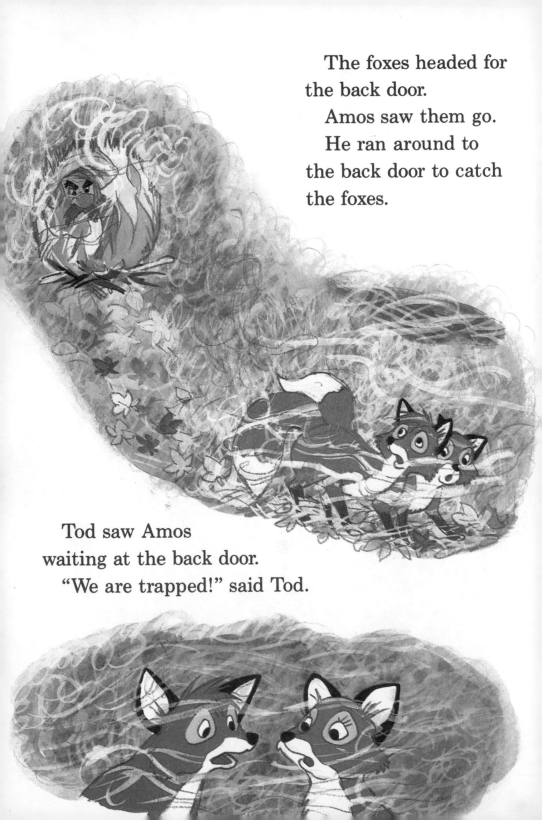

The foxes headed for
the back door.
Amos saw them go.
He ran around to
the back door to catch
the foxes.

Tod saw Amos
waiting at the back door.
"We are trapped!" said Tod.

"Go back the other way!" said Vixey.
The foxes dashed toward the fire.
They jumped over the flames and escaped
through the front door!

Tod and Vixey raced off.
They almost got away.
But Copper saw them and chased after them.
He was a good hunting dog now.

Amos ran after Copper.
But then he ran into some trouble.
Bear trouble!

The bear was feeling mean.
He knocked the gun out of Amos's hand.
"Help!" yelled Amos.
Copper came running.

Copper had to protect his master.
He jumped at the bear.
The bear raised his big paw...

...and hit
the dog.
Copper cried out in pain.

Tod heard Copper's cry.
He looked back.
He saw that his old friend
was in trouble.

Tod raced back to help Copper.

When the bear saw the fox,
he forgot about the dog.
He went straight for Tod.
Tod backed up—very slowly.

Tod backed onto a log.
The bear came after him.
The log ended over a river.
Now Tod had no place to go.

The log began to shake.

Tod could not hang on.
He fell into the river!

The bear slipped, too.
He landed in the river with a great splash.

The river carried the bear away.
It almost carried off Tod, too.
But Tod swam hard and reached land.

As Tod pulled himself out of the water,
Copper ran up to him.

"Thanks, Tod!" said Copper. "You saved
my life. That bear almost killed me!"

"You may be a hunting dog now," said Tod,
"but you are still my friend."

Just then Vixey
peeked out from behind
a nearby tree.

"Vixey, come and meet my old friend,
Copper," called Tod.

"Copper, this is my new friend, Vixey,"
said Tod. "We live in the burrow that
you found."

"I didn't know YOU were
in that burrow," said Copper.
"I'm sorry I chased you."

"Hey, Copper!" yelled
Amos. "Time to go home!"

Copper ran off to find Amos.
"Don't worry," he called back.
"I will never lead Amos to you again."
"Thanks," called Tod. "And if you
ever meet another bear, just yell!"

That night Tod and Vixey sat and talked.

"Do you think that you will ever see
Copper again?" asked Vixey.

"No," said Tod. "But we will not forget
each other. We are friends forever."

"You and I will be friends forever, too,"
said Vixey. "You can count on that!"